The Woodland Spies

Haunted House-Sitters

Kathy Foiles

VANTAGE PRESS
New York

This is a work of fiction. Any similarity between the names and characters in this book and any real person, living or dead, is purely coincidental.

Illustrated by Tanya Stewart

FIRST EDITION

All rights reserved, including the right of reproduction in whole or in part in any form.

Copyright © 2006 by Kathy Foiles

Published by Vantage Press, Inc.
419 Park Ave. South, New York, NY 10016

Manufactured in the United States of America
ISBN: 0-533-15189-9

Library of Congress Catalog Card No.: 2005901804

0 9 8 7 6 5 4 3 2 1

To Brandon, Lindsay, Chelsea, and Josh

1

Dear Chelsea,
 I am really having fun this summer. I am glad your Mom is watching me and Brandon. Did I tell you that I taught Max how to sit and shake hands? He is getting pretty good at his tricks. The next time we are solving a mystery, I'm sure he won't get in the way. Did you know old Mr. Hunter, from church, died? Mom said he died in his sleep. I bet he was 100 years old. I still liked him though. Well, gotta go. See you tomorrow.
 —Your cousin Lindsay

It was a hot July afternoon, and the three cousins were sitting around the swing set in Chelsea's backyard. They all lived in the same neighborhood, a small subdivision called Woodland Estates. Brandon and Lindsay's Mom and Dad both worked, so they stayed with Chelsea's Mom, their Aunt Kathy. Chelsea and Lindsay were both going into the fifth grade next year. Brandon would be in sixth.

The summer had started out pretty exciting with their first real mystery, "Buried Treasure." They had proven themselves to be good spies and were hoping for a lot of new cases to come their way. Unfortunately, none had.

"What do you want to do?" asked Brandon as he tossed a ball up in the air repeatedly. Brandon had brown hair and blue eyes. He was a little small for his age, but that didn't stop him from participating in all the sports their small town offered.

"Do you want to ride our bikes uptown?" asked Chelsea. Their subdivision was about two miles away from the town.

"We did that yesterday," moaned Brandon, "and there was nothing to do once we got there." He was right. Bridgeton, IL had one grocery store, two banks, two taverns and a small movie theater that usually ran movies that had come out last year. The one incentive for riding uptown was the Dairy Cream. That was a small ice cream shop in town. Other than that, a few local businesses and about five churches, there wasn't much up there.

"We could teach Max some new tricks," suggested Lindsay as she petted the dog. Max had came to stay with the Hawes about a month ago. He had been a stray their Dad brought home from work. Their Dad was a firefighter for Plainview Heights. That was a city about fifteen minutes away from Bridgeton.

"I'm tired of teaching Max tricks," said Chelsea. "You want to go out to the clubhouse? Joshua is asleep." Joshua was Chelsea's little brother. He was almost three and still took a nap every afternoon. The rest of the day he played with the kids and did his best to keep up with them.

"Nothing exciting ever happens out at the clubhouse anymore," said Lindsay. They had built the clubhouse earlier this summer after discovering a trail through the woods that led out to a big lake. That was where they became spies and solved their first mystery. However, Lindsay was right; the last couple of times they had been out there, it too had been pretty boring.

They finally decided to go around the front yard and play some ball. As they walked around the house Sheriff Akers was just pulling into the driveway. They all ran to meet him.

"Hey kids," he said as he got out of the car.

"Hi Sheriff Akers," they all said back.

"How's your summer goin'?" he asked.

"Actually, it's pretty boring," replied Chelsea.

"Boring! That's hard for me to believe, coming from you three."

"Well, believe it," said Brandon. "Got any good cases you want us to work on?"

"Well, as the matter of fact, I do have a job for you, if you're interested."

"We're interested," the kids said in unison, "what is it?"

"You all remember Mr. Hunter," he asked as he leaned against the car and cleaned his sunglasses. Chelsea watched him cleaning his glasses and thought about the game they play a lot were they compare people to dogs. They all had agreed once that Sheriff Akers was a bulldog. He appeared tough but they all knew better. He was a big man.

Lindsay thought his police uniform made him look bigger than he was. They had never seen him without his uniform on, but Chelsea assumed he looked as big in casual clothes.

"Sure," said Lindsay, "he went to our church."

"Well then I guess you also knew he passed away last week."

"Ya, my Mom said he died while he was sleeping," said Chelsea.

"That's right," said the Sheriff, putting his glasses back on.

"What's the mystery in that?" asked Brandon.

The Sheriff laughed. "I didn't say I had a mystery for you. I said I had a job for you."

"What kind of job?" asked Chelsea?

"Well, Mr. Hunter only had one son, Mark Hunter. You kids are probably too young to remember him. He hasn't lived in Bridgeton for many years. He lives in New York."

"Ya . . ." Lindsay said, getting impatient for the Sheriff to tell them what the job was.

"Well, I saw him at the funeral home the other night and he asked me if I knew of anyone that could watch his dad's house for awhile."

"Is he going to sell the house?" asked Chelsea.

"He has it listed with a realtor. You didn't let me finish. He also needs someone to take care of Mr. Hunter's cat."

"What is he going to do with the cat?" asked Lindsay.

"Mark wasn't sure. He couldn't take her with

him, and he didn't have the heart to send her to the pound. He just wants someone to stop by there every day and feed her. Just keep an eye on things until he gets back to settle the estate."

"And you want us to feed the cat," said Brandon disappointedly.

"Sorry it wasn't something more exciting," the Sheriff said with a laugh. "Are you interested?"

"We'll have to ask our parents first," said Lindsay, "but I'm sure they won't mind."

"It sounds good to me," said Chelsea, "I don't think my mom will care either."

The Sheriff looked at Brandon, who still had a look of disappointment on his face. "Oh ya," said the Sheriff, "did I mention the job pays $3.00 a day?"

Brandon's face lit up immediately. "Three dollars a day," he repeated. "We'll take it."

2

"Now remember to get the key from the police station," said Kathy Ellis, Chelsea's Mom. "Sheriff Akers said he left it with them."

"We know, we know," said Chelsea. "Then I will put it on this keychain and leave it in my pocket." She repeated the steps back that her mom had just gone over, for the third time.

"I just want to make sure you don't lose it," her mother said. "This is a big responsibility. I am proud of you three for taking it on." Chelsea's mom was a definite golden retriever, as the game went. She was tall and blonde and was always talking to them about the importance of being responsible and loyal. Chelsea's dad ran his own construction company. He worked a lot of hours. He was a German shepherd.

"Did Sheriff Akers tell you how long we would be doing this?" Lindsay asked her Aunt Kathy.

"No, it didn't sound like he was sure. I guess until Mark can get back to town to straighten things out."

"Come on," said Brandon as he walked out the front door. "We better get going."

"Be careful," Kathy called, "and watch for cars."

They could barely hear her. They were already down the front walk headed for their bicycles. Joshua was watching *Peter Pan* for the second time that day, and didn't even seem to notice them leaving. They compared Joshua to a miniature collie. He was very cute with his blond, curly hair and big dimples. However, he was also hyper.

They got on their bikes and peddled out of the subdivision. After making a right turn onto Blue Road they only had a short distance to go before they reached the big hill. There was only one hill all the way into town. But it was a big one. They all had to push their bikes up the other side. After that, it was smooth sailing and they were in town within ten minutes. They turned left on Main Street and Mr. Hunter's house came into view.

It was a big old house that sat on the corner of Main and Vine. It was a two-story house, unless you count the widow's walk. Then it would be three. Mr. Hunter had always taken good care of it, but the past few years it had started to look a little run down. They got off their bikes in front of the house.

"You know," said Lindsay, "this house looks like something off of a scary movie."

Lindsay was tall and skinny and much more the worrier of the three. Chelsea and Brandon had both agreed she was an Afghan hound. Her light brown hair had just a hint of red in it. Lindsay saw herself more as a collie.

"I never really thought about it before," said Chelsea, "but you're right."

"Maybe it's haunted," said Brandon, "a lot of old houses are."

"They are not," said Lindsay. "All that stuff is made up."

"How do you know?" said Brandon.

"Because I don't believe in ghosts, so they have to be made up."

"Ya, neither do I," said Brandon as he walked up to the front door. "But I wish this one was. That way this job might seem a little more exciting."

Brandon had claimed his likeness to be that of a Doberman pinscher. The girls didn't argue the fact but later secretly agreed it would have to be a miniature Doberman. He and Lindsay had a lot of the same features, however, people kept telling him if he didn't start growing, Lindsay was going to pass him up.

"Excuse me," said Chelsea. "I believe we have forgotten something." Lindsay and Brandon turned around and looked at her and then they all said together, "THE KEY."

They laughed as they rode up to the police station to pick up the key. They all agreed not to tell Chelsea's mom they had forgotten, even after she had reminded them so many times.

The police station was only a couple of blocks away and they were there in a few minutes. The officer behind the desk had the key in his desk drawer. "Sheriff Akers told me you would be in for this," he said as he handed them the key. "So you're going to take care of Tabby are you?"

"Ya, just until Mr. Hunter's son sells the house and decides what to do with her," said Lindsay.

The police officer laughed. "That might be awhile. From the looks of that house it needs a lot of fixin' up. I doubt too many people are going to be interested."

They thanked the officer and rode back down to Vine Street. There were two arched gateways at the entrance to the yard. They were covered with honeysuckle vines. The gate squeaked as they opened it. The steps to the front porch were a little warped but looked safe. Chelsea was carrying the key on the key chain her mother had given her. She unlocked the door and quickly put the key back in her pocket so that she wouldn't lay it down somewhere inside accidentally. Her mother had told her to do that also.

They opened the door and walked in. None of the kids had ever been inside the house before and were anxious to look around. The front door opened into an open foyer and Tabby, an orange and white striped cat, immediately greeted them. She rubbed up against their legs and purred as they all petted her. She was a short-haired cat but looking down at her socks, Chelsea noticed she still shed quite a bit. "Aww, poor thing, she must really be lonely without Mr. Hunter."

"Let's find her food," said Lindsay and walked in the direction she assumed the kitchen was. They found the cat food in the cabinet. It wasn't hard, there wasn't much else in the cabinets beside cat

food. "Wow, what do you think old Mr. Hunter ate? All that is in here is cat food."

"I'm sure his son cleaned out most of the food before he left. He wouldn't want anything going bad," said Chelsea. Lindsay opened the refrigerator. "Yep you're right, Chelsea, there isn't anything in here either."

They rummaged through some drawers and found a can opener. They fed Tabby and got her some water. She wasn't interested in eating though. She just wanted to be petted. "Maybe if we sit down in the kitchen with her, she won't think we are going to leave and she'll eat," suggested Lindsay. They all sat down on the floor by her food bowl. She walked around them all a few times rubbing against them and purring. Finally she decided to eat. They sat on the floor.

The kitchen was a fairly large room. One wall was all brick and the stove sat back in it. There was a metal kitchen table and chairs next to a window that looked out into the backyard. The cabinets were all white with metal handles. The room looked like it had been remodeled somewhere along the line but could probably use it again.

"When Tabby gets finished eating let's look around upstairs," said Brandon. "Ya, I bet it's neat up there," added Lindsay.

"Do you think you can get all the way up to the top where the window walk is?" asked Chelsea.

Chelsea had been more difficult to describe when choosing a dog match. They had finally agreed she was more like a cat. Her blonde hair reached down to her waist and she was much too concerned about how she looked, to be your average ten year old. Her mom always said she wished she would worry as much about her room. Of course what really made them think of her as a cat was her curious nature.

"That's widow's walk," said Brandon, "but I don't know if you can get up there or not."

Tabby finally finished eating and they decided to look around.

From the kitchen you could either go into the living room, which is the way they came in, or into the dining room. The living room had wooden floors with a big area rug in the middle of the floor. There was a couch, with an afghan hung over the back of it. A rocking chair sat in one corner and an old worn out recliner was next to the couch. Tabby jumped up in the recliner as they entered the room.

"Is this your chair?" Lindsay asked her as she stroked her fur.

"Must be," said Chelsea.

"I bet that was Mr. Hunter's favorite chair," stated Brandon. "That's probably why she's sitting there."

From the living room they walked back into the foyer and across the hall. "What do you think this room was used for?" asked Lindsay. "It's awful dreary-looking."

The room was dark with heavy curtains up to the windows. There were a lot of straight back chairs in the room, real old-looking ones. In two of the corners there were plant stands with ferns growing in them. "How could anything grow in this dark room?" Lindsay asked.

"No kidding," added Chelsea. "This room gives me the creeps," she said as she walked back out and down the hallway to the dining room. The others followed. The dining room wasn't much to look at either. Very formal, and very dusty. "I take it Mr. Hunter didn't use this room much," commented Lindsay. There was a china cabinet up against one wall with some old-looking dishes in it. The table was dark wood and would seat six.

"Let's look around upstairs," said Brandon. They went back to the foyer and up the stairs. Tabby followed. The upstairs had three bedrooms. One bedroom had a very small bathroom off of it. "Why would anyone build a bathroom so small?" asked Brandon.

"You can hardly turn around in here."

"I bet it used to be a closet," suggested Chelsea. "I saw somebody on TV remodeling an old house like this one. They took a closet and turned it into a bathroom." The furniture in all of the rooms looked old.

"You know I've seen a lot of this kind of stuff downtown at the craft and antique shops. Mom is always telling us not to touch anything," said Lindsay. "We better be careful."

"I wonder how you get upstairs to the widow's walk?" asked Brandon.

"Try that door at the end of the hallway," suggested Lindsay. It was locked.

"Maybe it's not safe to go up there anymore," said Chelsea. "That's probably why they keep the door locked."

"Dang," said Brandon, "I wanted to check it out."

"We better get going," said Lindsay, "did anyone give Tabby water?"

Neither Brandon or Chelsea had, so they all went back downstairs and filled her water bowl up with fresh water.

They said good-bye to Tabby and closed the front door behind them. Chelsea took the key out of her pocket and locked the door. As they started down the front steps they were surprised to see Mrs. Norris coming through the gate. Mrs. Norris was a thin woman with graying hair. She was probably in her late 50s but seemed much older. The kids knew who she was but never really talked to her. She was very quiet and would usually pass you by without as much as a hello.

She was as surprised to see the kids as they were her. "I was looking for Mr. Hunter," she said.

The kids looked at each other. Was it possible she didn't know that Mr. Hunter had passed away. "Mark Hunter," she explained, sensing their confusion.

"Oh," said Brandon. "He isn't here, he lives in New York."

"I know that," she said. "I just assumed when I saw the house open that he was the one in it."

"He is paying us to take care of Tabby," Lindsay explained.

"Oh, I see," she said. "Do you know if he will be in town anytime soon?"

"No, we were just told to come every day until the house sells and he gets everything settled," said Brandon.

It was apparent something he said didn't set well with Mrs. Norris. "Until the house sells," she repeated. "Is he trying to sell the house already?"

"Mrs. Carter, from Carter Real Estate, is supposed to be putting a sign in the yard soon."

"I see," she said, and without even saying good-bye she turned around and left.

"That was odd," said Chelsea.

"I'll say. She's strange, she never looks happy," said Lindsay. "Mom says she's a busybody."

"What's that suppose to mean?" asked Chelsea.

"I think it means she likes to know everything that is going on around town, whether it concerns her or not."

"Oh," said Chelsea. "I wonder why she wanted to see Mr. Hunter's son?"

"Who knows," said Brandon. "Let's just get going before she comes back and stares at us with those beady eyes again."

They all laughed as they got on their bikes and started riding home. As they turned back onto Blue Road they caught a glimpse of Mrs. Norris going into the Bridgeton Museum. For a small town it was strange that they had their own museum. It was just a little one-room building but supposedly had a lot of interesting facts about the history of Bridgeton. None of the kids had ever been in it before.

"I wonder what she is going there for," questioned Chelsea.

"She probably lives there with the other ancient fossils," Brandon said with a grin. He was always proud of himself when he made a good joke. The two girls laughed.

"She reminds me of a poodle," said Chelsea continuing with their game. "Maybe it's her curly hair, or her long skinny nose."

"No way, she's more like a basset hound with those droopy eyes."

"Brandon, if Mom hears you talking about people like that you're going to get in trouble," said Lindsay.

"I was only joking," said Brandon. "Come on, I'll race you guys home."

3

Brandon and Lindsay rode their bikes over to Chelsea's house every day. Their mom used to drop them off on her way to work, but they needed their bikes to ride uptown. They would play games or watch TV most of the morning. After Josh went down for his nap, sometime after lunch, they would head for town. That was Chelsea's mom's idea. She said it would break up their day. They all knew she really liked having the house nice and quiet for a couple of hours.

"Let's get going," called Brandon, who was already out the door at 12:30.

"I'm coming," said Chelsea, "I just have to get the key." She took the key off of the hook in the kitchen, where they had decided to keep it, and slipped it into her pocket.

The three kids rode into town. "This isn't all that bad," said Lindsay. "I thought it would get boring after awhile."

"We've only been doing it three days, Lindsay," commented Brandon.

"I know, but I really like riding up here every day. It gives us something to do."

"Ya, I like it too," said Chelsea. "I wonder

what's going to happen to Tabby when Mr. Hunter's son sells the house?"

"I wish we could take her," said Lindsay, "but I don't think Max would appreciate it very much."

"No, probably not," said Chelsea. "My dad doesn't like cats, so I know I could never keep her."

"I'm sure he'll find a good home for her," said Brandon. "I just hope it takes him awhile."

They parked their bikes in front of the old house and walked through the big iron gate. As Chelsea was getting the key out of her pocket they heard something inside the house.

"What was that?" asked Lindsay.

"I don't know, sounds like Tabby might have knocked something over." Chelsea unlocked the door and they went inside. Tabby ran out to meet them and immediately started purring.

"Hi, Tabby," Chelsea said as she leaned over to pet the cat. "Have you been up to mischief?" The cat rubbed up against her and continued purring.

The kids looked around but didn't notice anything unusual. "Oh well, I guess you're off the hook this time," Lindsay said stroking the cat. They fed her and checked all the windows downstairs. Yesterday they had found a window open in the kitchen.

"I wonder if we should have called the realtor about her leaving the window open yesterday," said Lindsay.

"I'm sure she just forgot," said Chelsea.

"Anyway it didn't hurt anything," said Brandon.

"I know, but it could have if it would have rained or something. She needs to be more careful."

"Well, everything looks okay today," said Chelsea. "You want to hang around for awhile and play with Tabby?"

"We might as well, we don't have anything else to do," said Brandon.

Lindsay took a couple of deep breaths. "Do you guys smell something?" Brandon and Chelsea both lifted their noses in the air and breathed in.

"I don't," said Brandon.

"What about you, Chelsea? Do you smell that?"

Chelsea smelled the air again. "You know, I think I do smell something. It smells like perfume."

"Where's it coming from?" asked Lindsay getting up and walking toward the living room. The other two followed with their noses in the air trying to follow the scent.

Once they were in the living room Brandon smelled it also. "I think it's coming from upstairs."

"Oh no," said Chelsea. "Maybe that's what we heard. Maybe Tabby knocked something over upstairs." They all ran up the stairs to check it out. Tabby followed.

They checked all the rooms but nothing was spilled in any of them. They walked into what had been Mr. Hunter's bedroom.

"Oh man, it really smells strong in here," said Brandon holding his nose.

Chelsea lifted her shirt over her nose. "It's got to be Mr. Hunter's cologne. I remember him smelling like that when we sat behind him at church."

"Ya, me too," added Lindsay. "It must be turned over in here somewhere for it to smell so strong."

The kids looked everywhere but never did find a spill. They opened the bedroom window and let the room air out. Chelsea looked at the dresser. There was a man's jewelry box on it, a small basket with loose change thrown in it, and a lamp. She walked across the hall and into the other bedroom that had a bathroom in it. She opened the medicine cabinet. She didn't want to be nosy, but she wanted to know where that smell had come from. There was a bottle of Old Spice inside. She took it down but didn't even need to open the lid. "Whew," she said out loud. "This is the stuff all right." The other two came in the bathroom.

"Did you find it?" asked Lindsay.

"I found a bottle of his cologne, but it wasn't spilled. It was sitting in the medicine cabinet with the lid on."

"That can't be it then," said Lindsay. "Maybe there is another bottle."

"I don't know," said Brandon, "but we better get going. It's almost three o'clock." They put the cologne back in the cabinet and closed the door. Brandon closed the bedroom window and locked it.

They said good-bye to Tabby, after making sure she had plenty of water, and left.

As Chelsea locked the door behind her she said, "Tomorrow we should change her kitty litter or there will be a different kind of smell in the house." They all laughed.

"That sure was strange," said Lindsay. "I don't understand how cologne sitting in a cabinet could smell up the whole house."

"Maybe Mr. Hunter's ghost did it," said Brandon, as he got on his bike.

"Stop it, Brandon."

"Maybe he doesn't think we are doing a good enough job taking care of Tabby so he came back to do it himself."

"Right, Brandon," said Lindsay, "and I guess he put some cologne on to make a good impression on us."

They rode to the end of the street and turned on Main. They passed Mrs. Norris who was walking in the opposite direction. She gave them a funny look and turned away. When they had rode a little ways Brandon said, "He was probably putting on cologne because he has a hot date with Mrs. Norris."

Lindsay laughed at the joke but couldn't help but wonder . . .

4

The next day Chelsea's mom came back from the mailbox with a letter from Mr. Hunter's son, Mark. It was addressed to Chelsea. Chelsea opened the letter immediately and read out loud.

Dear Chelsea, Brandon, and Lindsay,
  I just wanted to thank you for taking care of Tabby for me. You came highly recommended by Sheriff Akers. I will not be able to make it back for at least another week, maybe two. I hope you can continue to watch over things for me until then. I will be calling you in a few days to make sure everything is O.K.
  I have enclosed a check for the first week. Thanks again.

Mark Hunter

  Chelsea held up a check for $21.00.
  "Alright," said Brandon, snatching the check from her hand. "That's $7.00 each, let's cash it today when we go uptown."
  "Wait a minute, Brandon," said Lindsay. "We have only been feeding Tabby for four days, counting today. We should have only gotten a check for $12.00."

Brandon looked disgusted. "Big deal, Lindsay, he probably thought it would take the letter longer to get here." Then he looked at Chelsea's mom, who had been standing there listening to the letter. "It's okay if we cash the check isn't it, Aunt Kathy?"

"I don't see why not. Who is it made out to?"

Brandon looked at the check. "It's made out to you," he answered her.

She took the check from him and signed the back of it. "I'm sure you won't have any trouble at the bank," she said as she handed it back to him.

"Alright, let's go," he said, eager to get his hands on the money.

"Where is Joshua, Mom?" asked Chelsea.

"He's outside with Justin. I'm watching him today while his mom goes to the doctor."

"Who's Justin?" asked Lindsay?

"I used to work with his mom at the bank. Him and Josh are only a few months apart in age and they play pretty good together," her Aunt Kathy answered.

"Then it's okay if we leave early today?" asked Chelsea.

"Ya go ahead."

Brandon put the check in his pocket carefully and they all went out to the garage to get their bikes. They stopped at Main Street and waited for some traffic to pass. "Let's go to the bank first," said Brandon.

"That's the wrong way. Let's feed Tabby first. Then we can cash the check," said Lindsay.

Brandon and Lindsay were just about to start arguing when Chelsea piped up. "How about this. Why don't we take care of Tabby first, cash the check and then go to the Dairy Cream to celebrate our first paycheck."

"I like the way you think," said Brandon raising his eyebrows.

They turned left on Main and rode to Mr. Hunter's house. Chelsea unlocked the door and they went inside. For some reason Tabby didn't come running to meet them. They called her several times. Still no Tabby.

"Where could she be," said Lindsay worriedly.

"She's got to be around here somewhere," said Brandon. They went upstairs and called for her some more. She was nowhere to be found. They were debating on who was going to go down to the basement and look for her when Chelsea hollered, "There she is." She was pointing out the window to the backyard.

"She's outside," said Lindsay in disbelief. "How would she get outside?"

"I don't know," said Chelsea as she unlocked the back door and walked out, "but there she is."

At the sound of Chelsea's voice the cat looked up from her nap and meowed. The kids walked over to her. There she was laying in the middle of a flower bed filled with wildflowers. The kids all sat down and petted her. She began purring. They were as glad to see her as she was to see them.

"Tabby, how did you get out here?" said

Lindsay. "We could have lost our job if something would have happened to you."

"I bet that stupid realtor let her out," said Brandon. "We are going to have to say something. First the window and now this. What if she would have ran off."

"Brandon's right," added Lindsay. "You ought to call her and ask her about it Chelsea."

"Me! Why me?" asked Chelsea.

"You're good at that kind of stuff," said Brandon as he looked around the garden for the first time. "Wow, would you look at this place. There must be a hundred different kinds of flowers in here."

The kids all stood up and looked around. There was a statue of a woman holding a vase, in the middle of the garden. There were several large circular flower beds filled with all kinds of flowers. Little pebble sidewalks weaved in and out of the flower beds. There were a few weeds but for the most part it was very well taken care of. At the back of the property was an old garage.

"He must have spent a lot of time out here taking care of this," observed Lindsay.

Tabby rolled around in the flower bed looking very content. Chelsea looked at her. "I bet Tabby spent a lot of time out here with him," she said. "I bet she misses him."

The kids sat down next to her and Chelsea stroked the cat's fur again. "I sure hope they find a good home for her," Chelsea said.

"I don't think she wants a new home," said Brandon. "I think she wants to stay right here."

They all watched the cat as a grasshopper caught her eye and she got ready to pounce on it. "I still don't know why I should be the one to talk to the realtor," said Chelsea, getting back to the matter at hand.

"Okay, okay, we will go up together," said Lindsay.

"Right after we cash the check and get some ice cream," added Brandon.

"We better get Tabby inside and feed her, it's hard telling how long she's been out here," said Chelsea. They walked inside and Lindsay got her food out.

"Chelsea, while Lindsay takes care of Tabby, why don't we make sure all the windows are closed and that there isn't any way she could have gotten out on her own," said Brandon.

"Good idea, let's go."

The two cousins checked all the windows and doors, upstairs and down. All of them seemed to be shut tight and locked.

"It had to be the realtor," said Chelsea as they said good-bye to Tabby and locked the door behind them.

"Unless . . ." Brandon said with a grin.

"Don't start with the ghost thing again, Brandon," said Lindsay.

"Alright, alright, let's go."

They rode up town to the bank to cash the

check. The ice cream shop was only a couple of blocks away from the bank so it only took a few minutes to get there. They went inside to order. Brandon got a sherbet twist, which looks like a popsicle but is actually two different flavors of sherbet frozen on a stick. His favorite was orange and cherry. Lindsay got a twist cone and Chelsea settled for a chocolate milk shake. They were just about to take them outside and sit on the picnic table when they overheard a conversation about Mr. Hunter. They looked at each other and without saying a word they moved over to an empty table and sat down.

The ice cream shop was small and it was easy to hear any conversation no matter where you were sitting. Two women were sitting in the corner.

"Why that old house was believed haunted years ago. Now that it's empty again, it's all going to start back up." The woman continued.

A man and a woman sat at a table next to the ladies and it was apparent they too were eavesdropping on their conversation. The man laughed out loud and the woman nudged him to be quiet.

"I suppose you don't believe the old Hunter house is haunted, Mr. Dilley," one of the women said to him.

"Why that house is no more haunted than this ice cream shop," he replied.

"Well then how do you explain all the strange goings on here of late," she snipped.

"What's going on?" asked the man with a laugh.

"Why just last night I drove by there and saw light on the second floor," said one of the ladies.

"That's right," piped in the other woman, "and when I was walking by Monday night that same light was on, and I saw a shadow of someone up there."

"Well they probably have the lights on a timer," said the man. "Who is taking care of the place anyway?"

"I hear tell the realtor over on Fifth Street. What's her name, Imagene?"

"Renee Carter," the woman called Imagene answered. "At least that's who put the sign in the yard early this morning."

"Now you see," said the man as he got up to leave. "That's probably all there is to it."

"You think what you will," the woman said. "I've seen plenty of hauntings in my day, and I say it's a ghost."

The man laughed as he and his companion got up and left. The kids listened intently without saying a word.

The women continued their gossip but the subject soon changed and the kids decided to sit outside after all. As they were opening the door to go out, they ran into Paul Manns. Paul was the youth minister at their church.

"Hi guys," he said. "How's it goin?" Paul was a great guy. He planned all of the youth events at the

church. Except the most recent one, which was a surprise birthday party for Paul. He turned twenty-five. The youth had planned the entire party. There were twenty-five balloons, twenty-five guests, and, of course, twenty-five candles. They all loved being able to do something special for him. Chelsea and Lindsay had both noticed the way some of the older girls started helping out with the youth after Paul joined the church.

"Fine," they replied. "We were just going to sit outside on the picnic table."

"Sounds good, can I join you?"

"Sure."

"I'll meet you out there." He went on in and ordered while the kids walked around the side of the building and sat down. There were two old tables out there. One was under a roof and the other sat out in the open. Lindsay and Chelsea sat at the sunny table while Brandon hopped up on the other.

"Do you think we should tell Paul about the strange things happening at Mr. Hunter's house?" asked Lindsay.

"No, I don't want people thinking we're afraid," said Brandon. "Besides those two old ladies just like to gossip. None of that stuff is true."

Just then Paul came around the side of the building carrying a vanilla cone. "None of what stuff is true?" he asked.

"Oh, we heard some ladies inside talking about Mr. Hunter's house being haunted," answered

Chelsea. "We don't believe any of that stuff though," she quickly added.

"Oh ya, I almost forgot. You guys are taking care of Mr. Hunter's cat. How's that going?"

"Good," said Brandon. "We're celebrating our first paycheck with this ice cream."

"Hey, congratulations," he said. "How long do you think this job will last you?"

"We're not sure," said Lindsay. "Mr. Hunter's son doesn't think he will be back in town for awhile."

"Well, that works out good for you guys," he said as he licked his melting ice cream cone. "So what's this about the house being haunted?"

"Oh it's nothing," said Brandon. "Those ladies said they keep seeing lights and shadows upstairs."

"Oooooo," Paul said with big eyes. "It must be haunted."

They all laughed. "You guys haven't seen anything strange around there have you?" he asked.

"Well . . ." Lindsay said.

"No," said Brandon at the same time.

Paul raised his eyebrows and wrinkled his forehead the way he always does when something they say or do doesn't make sense. They laughed. He looked at Chelsea. "How about you. Have you seen anything strange happening?"

"Well, not really strange. Sometimes a window is open when we get there, and we know we didn't leave it open."

"Ya and then one day the whole house smelled like Mr. Hunter's cologne," Lindsay chimed in. "We thought Tabby had spilled a bottle accidentally, but we could never find one."

"Hmmmm," Paul said raising one eyebrow, "anything else?"

"The worst thing happened today," Chelsea said. "When we got there we couldn't find Tabby anywhere. Come to find out, she was out in the garden taking a nap. All the doors were locked and so were the windows."

"Wow, that is strange," said Paul. "What do you think?"

"We figure it's the realtor not being careful," said Brandon. "We're going to go and see her and make sure she remembers to be careful not to let Tabby out."

"I think that sounds like a good idea," said Paul. "And as far as the women go in the ice cream shop . . ." he ate the last bite of his cone, "I wouldn't put much thought into that."

"We weren't," said Chelsea as she tossed her empty cup in the trash can. "We better get going if we're going to see the realtor," she added. "Mom will be starting to worry."

They all walked around to the front of the building where their bicycles were at. "You guys let me know if anything else happens. I love a good mystery," Paul said with a laugh.

They agreed to keep him posted and rode off. Carter Realty was across the railroad tracks and a few blocks away from Blue Road, so it was actually on the way. They parked their bicycles out front and walked in. Chelsea had agreed to do the talking as long as the other two went in with her.

"We're looking for Renee Carter," she said timidly to the receptionist.

"I'm Renee," said a voice from across the room. "What can I do for you?" She was a tall woman with blondish brown hair. She wore a navy blue skirt and jacket and looked like she was just getting ready to leave.

"I'm Chelsea Ellis, and these are my two cousins, Brandon and Lindsay Hawes," she said.

"Oh, you're the kids taking care of Mr. Hunter's cat," she said with a smile.

"Ya, that's right," said Chelsea, relieved she knew who they were.

"What can I do for you?" she asked a second time.

"We weren't sure you knew Tabby was still living in the house. We were going to ask you to be careful not to let her out when you come in."

"Oh, sure thing, I'll be careful," she smiled and walked toward her desk.

"Well, that's all we wanted," said Chelsea.

"Okay," the realtor said without looking up. "I'll probably start showing the house in a couple of days."

The kids stopped and looked at each other. "You mean you haven't shown the house to anyone yet?" asked Lindsay.

"No not yet, but I have several people interested in it because of its historical background. I can't wait to get over there and take a look at it."

The kids shared the same look again. "You mean you haven't even been in the house yet?" inquired Brandon.

"No, I've just been too busy, but I'll get over there tomorrow or the next day for sure."

The kids started to walk out again when Chelsea thought of something. "Is it possible someone else has been in the house."

"No, I have the only key and nobody has asked me for it. Why do you ask?"

"Well, the cat got out today and we just thought maybe someone from here accidentally let her out," said Chelsea.

"No, nobody from here."

"Okay, thanks," they said and walked outside.

"Well, there goes that theory," said Chelsea as they got on their bikes.

"There has got to be a logical explanation," said Brandon. "Someone is playing tricks on us."

"Who would do that," asked Lindsay, "and why?"

"I don't know," said Brandon slowly, "but it looks as if we've got ourselves another mystery."

5

"Chelsea," her mother called, "Mark Hunter is on the phone for you." Chelsea ran to the phone.

"Hello," she said politely.

"Chelsea, hi, this is Mark Hunter. How are things going?" He sounded like he might be on a car phone or maybe a speaker phone. The connection was not very clear.

"Everything is going fine," Chelsea said. "Tabby is doing good also."

"Great, I was told you kids were responsible."

Chelsea debated over telling him about the strange things that had been happening.

"Have you found a home for Tabby yet?" she inquired.

"No, I haven't had a chance to do anything yet. I'm hoping to be home in a week or two. My realtor tells me she has several people interested in the house."

"Yes, that's what she told us also."

"You've talked to the realtor?"

"Well, yesterday we went by her office. We thought she might have let Tabby out by accident. We found her in the garden."

"Oh, I see," he said. Chelsea could hear papers

rustling in the background. She figured he was only half listening to her.

"But the realtor said she hadn't been in the house. We're not sure how Tabby got out. We are always very careful when we leave to make sure the doors are all locked."

"Oh, I'm sure you are. Don't worry about it. That's an old house and it needs a lot of repairs. The cat probably knows a way out."

"Ya, I guess you're right," Chelsea said.

"Well, I gotta run. Keep up the good work."

"We will, thanks." They hung up. Chelsea thought about their conversation. *It is an old house. Maybe Tabby does know a way out.* They should check over everything more carefully, even the basement. That was a job nobody wanted, but it needed to be done. She decided she would discuss this with Brandon and Lindsay first thing.

The kids had been invited to a swim party that afternoon by Alesha Cato. She didn't live far from Mr. Hunter's house so they had decided to wear their swimming suits under their clothes when they rode uptown that day. The party was to start at 2:00 P.M. As soon as lunch was over, they got their stuff together. It took a while to get their towels tied to their bikes but they managed.

"You know," Chelsea said as they rode, "I really think we need to investigate that basement."

"No way," said Lindsay. "It's probably full of spiders and cobwebs."

"Well I think Mr. Hunter's son might be right.

What if Tabby did get out through a broken window or something down there. We don't want her running off."

"Ya, Chelsea's right," Brandon chimed in. "It will only take a minute to go down there."

They parked their bikes on the sidewalk and opened the iron gate. As Chelsea was putting the key in the lock they heard something inside.

"What was that?" she whispered.

"I don't know, but hurry up so we can catch someone if they're in there," said Brandon.

Chelsea opened the door quickly but didn't move in. They all stood just inside the doorway and listened. There was complete silence. They looked around the room cautiously, then slowly they walked in further.

"Do you see anything unusual?" Chelsea asked in a whisper.

"No," Brandon whispered back. "I'm gonna look in the kitchen." He walked in the kitchen and Chelsea slowly walked up the stairs. She had just gotten to the top step when she heard Lindsay holler out.

"You guys, come here quick!"

Brandon and Chelsea both ran back into the living room. "What is it?" they both asked at the same time.

"Look," said Lindsay and pointed toward the recliner chair. Tabby sat curled up in the chair looking perfectly content.

"What," said Chelsea. "It's just Tabby sitting in a chair."

"Not the chair, the table next to the chair."

Brandon and Chelsea both looked at the table. A tea cup and saucer were sitting on the table . . . full of tea.

"Where did that come from?" asked Brandon.

"I don't know, it was just sitting there," replied Lindsay.

Chelsea leaned over and felt the cup. Her eyes grew wide. "It's hot," she whispered.

The cousins stared at the cup of hot tea for several minutes before anyone said anything. "Someone was in here," said Brandon, "we heard them."

"But where did they go?" questioned Lindsay.

"And why would someone come in here, fix a cup of hot tea and then run off?" said Chelsea.

"I'll tell you why," said Brandon. "To scare us. Someone wants us to think this house is haunted, and I'm not buying it."

"Why would someone do that?" asked Lindsay. "And how do they get in and out?"

"That's what we need to find out," said Chelsea. "From now on when we get here I'll come in the front door as usual. Brandon, you go around back to see if anyone comes out that way, and Lindsay, you stay out on the sidewalk. That way we ought to have every angle covered. If someone is leaving the house as we come in, we'll see them."

"That's a good plan. I wish we would have thought of it yesterday," said Brandon.

"Ya, me too," said Lindsay. "Then we would already have caught them."

"Let's look around and make sure everything else looks okay," suggested Chelsea.

"Okay but we can't take long, we're supposed to be at Alesha's at two o'clock."

The kids looked around and fed Tabby. Nothing seemed to be out of place. Lindsay brought the cup of tea in from the living room and washed it in the sink.

"Let's get going," Brandon said.

"What about the basement, we haven't been down there yet," said Chelsea.

"I tried to turn the light on, but the bulb must be burnt out," said Brandon. "We'll bring a flashlight tomorrow and check it out."

"Okay," said Chelsea. "Let's get going."

They locked the door behind them but not before double checking the back door. "Whoever is getting in here must have a key of their own. This door is locked tight," said Chelsea. They went back out to the front and got on their bikes. They were just getting ready to leave when Mrs. Norris walked by.

"Hello," she said, "how are things going?"

"Fine," Lindsay answered her.

"It is a magnificent house, isn't it," she said looking up at the old house admiringly. The kids all looked at each other unsure of what to say, or why she was even talking to them.

"It's nice," said Chelsea.

"It has such historical value," Mrs. Norris continued. "Did you know this house was built in the 1800s?"

"No, we didn't," Chelsea said. "I guess that's what Mrs. Carter meant the other day when she said she had a lot of people interested in it for historical reasons."

Mrs. Norris looked sharply at Chelsea. "Did you say she had a lot of people interested in it?"

"That's what she said," Chelsea continued. "She is supposed to start showing the house today or tomorrow."

"I see," said Mrs. Norris, who seemed to be her old self again. "It would certainly be a shame to see someone get a hold of a house like this that didn't have respect for it." Once again she stared up at the house. The kids looked at each other and shrugged their shoulders.

"We've got to go," said Brandon, as he started to peddle off. "Bye," the girls said as they followed him. Mrs. Norris didn't answer. She just kept staring at the house.

"I think she's creepier than anything that's happened in that house," said Lindsay.

"Me too," added Chelsea. "She sure seems to know a lot about the house though."

"You think she has something to do with all the strange things happening?" questioned Lindsay.

"I wouldn't think so," said Chelsea, "but she sure seems to be around a lot."

"Did you notice the way she looked at you, Chelsea, when you mentioned Mrs. Carter having interested buyers?" asked Brandon as they turned into Alesha's driveway.

"Did I . . . I thought she was putting a hex on me for a minute." They all laughed as they got off of their bikes and untied their towels.

"Let's not mention anything to anyone at the party," Brandon suggested.

"Good idea, we don't want to spread any more rumors around about the house being haunted," said Lindsay.

The party was a lot of fun. There were probably eight other kids there they knew from either church or school. They had races and a diving contest. Alesha's Mom came out of the house with lemonade and cookies about 4:30. The kids all got out of the pool for a snack. As they sat around the picnic table eating, one of the kids, Kasandra Brown, brought up Mr. Hunter's house.

"That place gives me the creeps," she said. "My mom says there have been stories about it being haunted for years."

"Ya and ever since old Mr. Hunter died," added Adam, a boy Brandon's age, "strange things have started happening again."

"What kind of things?" Brandon asked.

"Lights flickering on and off."

"Shadows walking around upstairs."

"I heard someone even say they heard chains rattling when they walked by one night."

Almost everyone there had a story to tell about the old house. The cousins listened to them all, not mentioning a word about their taking care of Tabby. They heard all kinds of stories that ranged from screams in the middle of the night to one kid saying he saw Mr. Hunter sitting on the porch swing. That's where Brandon drew the line.

"That's the most ridiculous thing I've ever heard," Brandon said. "You didn't see Mr. Hunter sitting on the porch."

The boy was caught off guard. "Well, maybe I didn't, but I heard someone in the grocery store say they did."

"Well, they're full of beans too," said Chelsea. "I can't believe you guys believe all those stories."

"You don't?" they all asked.

"Of course not," said Lindsay. "We don't believe in ghosts."

"Hey," said Adam squinting his eyes as if trying to remember something. "Didn't I see you guys leaving Mr. Hunter's house the other day?"

"Maybe," said Brandon, now wishing he hadn't said anything.

"What were you doing there?" he asked.

The kids looked at each other for a second and then Lindsay spoke. "We are taking care of Tabby, Mr. Hunter's cat."

A hush fell over the hungry kids who had been talking non stop a minute ago. "You mean you go in that house every day?" asked Alesha with wide eyes.

"Of course we do," said Chelsea, "and believe me, there are no ghosts in it."

"Well even so," said Alesha, "you wouldn't catch me in there in a million years."

"Ya, you guys must be some sort of weirdos goin' into a place like that," Adam added.

"Maybe we're just not scardy cats like you guys," Lindsay said.

"Ya, and maybe the next time you go in . . ." said Alesha, "you won't come out." After the last comment, Alesha's mom came outside to clean up. "What are you guys talking about?" she asked.

"Brandon, Lindsay, and Chelsea are all taking care of Mr. Hunter's cat," said Alesha.

Alesha's mom quickly tried to hide the surprised look on her face. "Oh, that's nice."

"Mom, don't you think that place is haunted?"

"You can't put any faith in those stories, Alesha," her mother said. "People like to tell stories like that and if they are not interesting enough, they add something to them."

"Well, I guess," said Alesha, "but you still wouldn't catch me going in there."

It was almost five o'clock by now and some of the kids were getting ready to leave. "We better go too," said Brandon. The three cousins got up and picked up their towels. They were tying them onto their bicycles when Alesha came out front to talk to them.

"Hey, I'm sorry about what we said, we didn't mean anything by it."

"That's okay," said Chelsea, "everybody is entitled to their own opinion."

"Ya, I guess so," Alesha said. "I'm glad you came to my party."

"Thanks for inviting us," said Lindsay. "Ya, thanks," Brandon and Chelsea added.

"See ya later," Alesha said as she waved good-bye.

"See ya," the cousins hollered back.

They rode home quietly. Each one thinking of the different stories they had heard about the house. Were they the only ones in the entire town that didn't think the house was haunted? It was up to them to solve this mystery and let the whole town know that there is no such things as ghosts.

6

Sunday they all went to church as usual. Both of their families went to the First Baptist Church of Bridgeton. As Chelsea and Lindsay were walking to their class on the second floor, they passed Paul Manns on his way downstairs.

"Hey girls," he said with a smile. "How's the house-sitting going?"

"Okay," they said in unison.

"Made enough money to buy me an ice cream yet?" he asked jokingly.

"Not quite," said Lindsay, as they walked around him, "but we'll let you know." He laughed as he hurried down the stairs. The Hawes's had a family reunion to go to that day, on their dad's side, so Chelsea had agreed to take care of Tabby herself. The Ellis's all stopped at Mr. Hunter's house on their way home from church and waited while Chelsea ran in to feed her. Nothing seemed out of place that day but Chelsea wasn't wasting much time looking around. Not only were her parents and Josh waiting for her in the car, but she felt just a little uneasy about being in the house alone. She quickly fed Tabby, gave her fresh water, and promised to stay longer the next day.

Monday morning, on their way uptown, Chelsea told Brandon and Lindsay an idea she had last night.

"Why don't we stop at the museum on our way to feed Tabby today?" she asked.

"Why?" inquired Brandon.

"I've never been in it before," said Chelsea, "but Mrs. Lewis came to school last year and told us about it."

"Oh ya, I remember her," chimed in Lindsay. "She gave a talk on the history of Bridgeton."

"Ya, that's her," said Chelsea. "Maybe she could shed some light on all these rumors about Mr. Hunter's house. Remember yesterday, Mrs. Norris said it was built in the 1800s. I bet we can find a lot of information up there."

"Okay, as long as it doesn't take too long," said Brandon. "It's already hot out here and the longer we're in town, the hotter it's gonna get."

They parked their bikes in front of the small museum and walked in. Mrs. Lewis was sitting at a small table in the back of the room doing a crossword puzzle. She looked up as they came in and smiled at them. "Hello," she welcomed, "can I help you?"

"We would like some information about some of the historical homes in town," said Chelsea politely.

"Any house in particular?" she asked, as she stood up and walked toward them.

"Yes, the house on the corner of Main and Vine . . . Mr. Hunter's house," answered Lindsay.

"Oh, the old Hill house," she said mysteriously. "Well, you've come to the right place. I can tell you all kinds of things about that house."

The kids all smiled. Mrs. Lewis was a very nice older lady, probably in her late 60s. She had gray hair fixed up nicely on her head. Chelsea had seen her leaving the beauty shop uptown many times. She wore glasses with red frames and was always dressed nicely. She sounded like she would be a good story teller.

"That house was built in 1828 by Dr. Walter Hill," she started. "Mr. Hill was strongly against slavery. He was a very prominent figure in the underground railway."

"The what?" asked Brandon.

"The underground railway," she repeated "was the escape route for many slaves from the South who were trying to escape to the North where they would be set free."

"They actually had a railroad under the town?" Brandon asked wide-eyed.

"Well not exactly," she continued. "However they did have many hiding places in their homes where they would hide slaves until it was safe for them to move on."

"Hiding places," questioned Lindsay. "You mean like under the bed?"

"No, no, some of them had tunnels under their house where they could hide the slaves. Others had hidden rooms. Who knows, maybe they did hide a few under the bed," she laughed.

"Did Mr. Hunter's house have any hidden tunnels?" asked Chelsea.

"Hmm, let's see," she said thinking out loud. She walked over and pulled a book off of one of the shelves and thumbed through it. She read for a few minutes. "No I don't believe it did," she finally answered. "Although I have heard rumors, but I don't think anything was ever found."

"There were a lot of ghost stories associated with that house though," she said with a smile. "Would you like to hear one of them?"

"Ya," they all said at the same time.

"Well the story goes," she began in a whisper. "A long long time ago the house was used as a boarding house. Many of the guests complained of hearing a shot ring out in the wee hours of the night. An investigation proved that a mother had murdered her baby there one night.

"Even after the investigation one visitor said she could hear a baby crying down the hall most of the night."

The kids were wide-eyed as they listened to the story. "The rumors came and went over the years. There were reports of hearing chains rattling up and down the staircase and so on. I never put much stock in that sort of nonsense though," she said speaking back in her regular voice. "But they are fun to repeat. Why are you so interested in that particular house?" she asked.

"We are taking care of Mr. Hunter's cat, Tabby, for awhile," said Chelsea. "We were just curious."

"Well, you haven't seen any ghost yet have you?" she asked with a smile.

Chelsea and Lindsay were silent so Brandon spoke up. "No, nothing unusual."

"And I don't suspect you will," she said starting to put the book back on the shelf. Then she turned around and held out the book. "Would you like to take this with you?" she asked.

"Could we?" Chelsea asked.

"I don't think we'll miss it for a couple of weeks. I can trust you to bring it back, can't I?"

"Yes, ma'am," said Chelsea as she took the book. "I'll bring it back as soon as we're through with it."

"Take your time," Mrs. Lewis smiled. "You kids are the first visitors this old museum has seen in quite awhile. It's been nice talking to you."

"Thanks for all of your help," said Lindsay, as they turned to leave.

"No problem," she said. "You kids take care of yourself."

"We will," they said as they waved good-bye.

"Wow, I can't wait to read what else this book has to say about Mr. Hunter's house," said Chelsea.

"Me either," said Lindsay. "Maybe we will find out about a hidden room in the house or something."

"If there is a hidden room, maybe that's where someone has been hiding to play tricks on us while we're there."

"Ya, and if we can find the room . . ." They all

smiled at each other and peddled faster. They remembered their new plan for entering the house. Brandon went to the backyard, Lindsay stayed out on the sidewalk and Chelsea went in through the front door. Nothing seemed unusual and Chelsea called everyone in. Once they were inside they fed Tabby and looked around. They went through the house again but didn't see anything out of the ordinary.

"Let's get back to your house and read the book," said Lindsay to Chelsea. "Maybe tomorrow we will have a better idea of what to look for."

"Okay, let's go," said Chelsea. Even though the temperatures were in the middle nineties that day and the humidity was high, they peddled home quickly and without complaining. Their minds were preoccupied with what they might discover in the book.

As soon as they got home, they went straight to Chelsea's room and closed the door. It was soon opened again by Joshua. "You want to play with me, Brandon?" he asked his cousin.

"In a minute, Josh, Chelsea's going to read us something." Joshua took a seat on the floor next to Brandon and Lindsay waiting for the story. Chelsea started reading. It all seemed very boring as she skipped around the book looking for something interesting.

"You want to play with me now?" asked Josh again.

"Ya. I'll play with you," said Brandon. "Let me

know if you find anything interesting," he said to Chelsea.

Chelsea continued to look over the book and was about to give up when she hollered for the other two. "You guys come in here . . . I think I found something."

Brandon and Lindsay came into the room hurriedly followed by Joshua "What did you find?" they asked.

"Ya, what you find, sissy?" Josh asked her.

"Listen to this," Chelsea said, and began reading.

"The famous Hill house played a very important role in the Underground Railway. It had a tunnel underneath the house that led from the Hill house to the Hopper house north of town. This tunnel was part of an escape route used by fleeing slaves from the South."

"I thought Mrs. Lewis said there wasn't a tunnel," said Brandon.

"She did," answered Chelsea. "But maybe she doesn't know everything about the house."

"That would be so cool if we could find an underground tunnel," said Brandon.

"Ya cool," mimicked Josh. They all laughed.

"Let's check out the basement tomorrow," said Chelsea. "If we're gonna find something it would be down there."

7

They had been taking care of Tabby for seven days now. Each day seemed to get stranger and yet they had no clue as to what, or who, was messing around with things. They had tried and tried to figure out some possible explanations but had not been able to come up with anything. They got to the house and noticed as they were walking up the front walk that the door was open. They could hear people talking inside. They walked in to find Mrs. Carter showing the house to a middle-aged couple. They all looked up surprised when the kids walked in.

"Sorry," Lindsay said, "we didn't know you were in here."

"Oh, that's not a problem," Mrs. Carter said. "These are the three children that are looking after Mr. Hunter's cat," she explained to the couple. They smiled.

"Do whatever you need to do guys," Mrs. Carter said. "We were just on our way upstairs."

The couple was admiring the woodwork and the banister when they heard a loud noise. They all stood frozen waiting for the sound to come again. "What was that?" asked the man.

"I can't imagine," Mrs. Carter answered. Soon

the sound came again only this time it was more distinct. It sounded like chains rattling. It was coming from upstairs somewhere.

"What on earth . . ." Mrs. Carter said as she started up the stairs. The couple followed her with all three kids right behind them. They hurried upstairs, but by the time they got to the top of the stairs the ruckus stopped. They searched every room but nothing unusual was found.

"How do you get to the widow's walk?" the man asked.

"Let's see," said Mrs. Carter, "it must be around here somewhere."

"I think it's that door at the end of the hall," Brandon said, "but it is locked."

"Oh," said Mrs. Carter, "let's try one of these keys." She tried several until one opened the door. "Be careful," said Mrs. Carter, as the gentleman and his wife walked up there to look around. "I haven't been up there and I don't know how safe it is." They came back down shortly. "It's a great view," he said, "and it actually looks pretty sturdy."

"Can we look up there?" Brandon asked.

"Go ahead," said Mrs. Carter. "You don't get a chance to see something like this nowdays." The kids all walked up the stairs. There wasn't as much room up there as they had thought there would be. It was all open and a nice breeze blew through.

"This is really cool," said Chelsea.

"Ya," said Brandon, "you can see the whole town from here."

"We better get down you guys," said Lindsay. "I think they are waiting on us."

The cousins came down and Mrs. Carter relocked the door. The couple was still looking through the bedrooms.

"Did you see anything?" Mrs. Carter asked.

"Not a thing, I can't, for the life of me, imagine what was making that noise."

The kids all looked at each other but didn't say anything. The couple and Mrs. Carter continued to look around upstairs while the kids went back downstairs to feed Tabby.

"What do you make of that?" Brandon whispered, once they were down in the kitchen.

"I don't know," said Chelsea, "but at least we know we're not crazy. They all heard it."

"Ya, they heard it," said Lindsay, "but they couldn't explain it."

"We thought someone was trying to scare us," thought Brandon out loud. "Maybe it's not us they want to scare."

"What do you mean?" asked Chelsea.

"Maybe they want to scare off potential buyers."

"Why?"

"Shhh, here they come."

The kids put Tabby's food down and got her some water. Mrs. Carter brought the couple into the kitchen and was telling them about the beautiful garden. The man still seemed interested but his wife was looking over her shoulder a lot as she walked from room to room.

Just as they were about to go out the back door, they all heard a door slam shut upstairs. None of them moved or made a sound. A second later there were footsteps running down the stairs. The kids moved closer to each other, they were barely breathing. Several minutes went by. They all stood frozen in the kitchen. No one made a sound. Just when they thought the excitement might be over, the door to the basement, which is located in the kitchen, close to where they were standing squeaked open, just a little bit. The kids, still standing next to each other in somewhat of a huddle, moved away from the door. A cool breeze went through the room.

They turned and looked at Mrs. Carter and her buyers. The woman's face was white as a sheet and she looked as if she were going to pass out any minute.

"I need some air," she whispered and rushed out the back door.

"I think we've seen enough," the man said hurriedly and followed her.

Mrs. Carter went after them trying to explain that it's an old house and was probably just settling. The kids were left alone in the kitchen.

"You guys still don't believe in ghosts?" said Lindsay wide-eyed.

"It couldn't be a ghost," said Chelsea, as if she

were trying to convince herself. "There are no such things."

"Then how do you explain what just happened," said Lindsay still staring at the basement door.

"I hate to say this," said Brandon, "but there is only one way to find out." He picked up the flashlight off of the counter. They had brought it with them that day to check out the cellar.

"You're not going down there are you?" Lindsay whispered, as if not to alert the ghosts.

"That's exactly what I'm gonna do," he said and boldly walked over and opened the basement door. He shined his flashlight down the stairs. "You guys comin'?"

Chelsea and Lindsay looked at each other. Neither one wanted to, but they didn't want Brandon to go down alone. They slowly followed him down the dark staircase. It was musty smelling and felt damp. However, it wasn't as cold as the air that went past them a few minutes earlier. They stood on the stairs and shone the light around the small room. Not much was down there. Several old boxes full of junk sat off in one corner. A workbench with some old looking tools was against another wall and a wine rack sat against the third wall. Nothing was under the stairs.

"Nobody could have been down here," said Brandon. "There is nowhere to hide." He shone his light up higher on the walls. There was one small window, but it was unlikely an adult could squeeze through it.

"Do you think someone could fit through that window?" Chelsea suggested.

"I doubt it," said Brandon. "Maybe someone our size, but how would they reach it. They would need to stand on something and there is nothing under the window."

They looked around some more but never got off of the bottom step. Finally they agreed nothing was down there and returned to the kitchen. They closed the door but it wouldn't latch.

"What do you make of that?" said Brandon.

"A door at the top of the stairs could never be permanently latched," Lindsay slowly recited.

"What are you talking about?" asked Brandon.

"Remember that story Mrs. Lewis told us about the mother killing her baby and people hearing a baby cry in the middle of the night?"

"Ya, so," said Brandon.

"Well yesterday I was reading the book she lent us. It told that same story but it also said from that day on the door at the foot of the stairs could never be latched."

"This isn't at the foot of the stairs," observed Brandon.

"Maybe not now, but it could have been. Who knows what the house originally looked like," replied Chelsea. They all silently looked back at the basement door.

"Maybe we need to go home and read that book more thoroughly," suggested Chelsea.

"I'm all for that," agreed Lindsay, who was more than ready to get out of the house.

They looked for Mrs. Carter, but she and her clients had already gone. They locked the house up and left.

"I hope Tabby is okay," said Chelsea.

"None of this stuff seems to upset her," said Brandon, as he got on his bike.

"Maybe she's used to it," added Lindsay.

They all looked at each other, but no one commented on the last statement.

"Let's get out of here," said Brandon. "We've got our work cut out for us, if we're going to solve this mystery."

8

They arrived early Wednesday morning. They had been taking care of Tabby for nine days. Since their first trip to Mr. Hunter's, last Tuesday, many things had happened. They went over them all on their ride into town.

"First of all," Lindsay said, "somehow Tabby can get out of the house when all the doors and windows are locked."

"Either that or someone let her out," observed Chelsea.

"We definitely smelled Mr. Hunter's cologne in the house last week. I know we weren't imagining that," stated Lindsay.

"That was his cologne all right," replied Chelsea, "but we still don't know where it was spilled or how it got spilled."

"Don't forget about the cup of hot tea," said Brandon. "That's the most positive proof we have that someone has been in the house."

"And then last but not least, yesterday's incident," said Lindsay.

They all rode in silence as they thought about all that had went on in the house yesterday. The slamming doors, footsteps on the stairway and most chilling of all the cold breeze that swept through the kitchen after the basement door creaked open. They were still in deep thought as they parked their bicycles in front of Mr. Hunter's house and opened the iron gate.

"Oh hello," Mrs. Carter greeted them as she was coming out of the house. "I'll leave the door open for you since you're here. That cat has been meowing ever since I got here, but I never did see her. She might have got herself closed into a room or something."

"Thanks," Lindsay answered. "We'll find her."

Mrs. Carter turned and looked at the old house. "It sure is a beautiful old house," she said almost to herself. "It sure is a shame."

"What's a shame?" asked Brandon.

Mrs. Carter looked at him, then she looked at both girls. "You guys are something else. Didn't that whole episode yesterday scare you even a little?"

"Well, sure it did a little," said Lindsay.

"But here you are first thing in the morning ready to walk right back in there again."

"We have to," said Chelsea. "Who would feed Tabby?"

The realtor laughed. "I don't know whether to admire you guys or worry about you."

"I guess your buyers aren't very interested anymore," said Brandon.

"Not very interested," she said slowly and then laughed out loud. "Not only are they not interested anymore, I've had three canceled showings this morning. The word is out. Mr. Hunter might as well take it off the market."

"You mean they really think it's haunted?" Chelsea asked, unbelieving.

Mrs. Carter was through the gate and opening her car door. "I can't say I blame them, can you?" She got in her car and drove away.

The kids were still watching her drive off when something caught Brandon's eye. He turned and ran toward the backyard without saying a word.

"Stay on the front walk," said Chelsea to Lindsay, as she turned and hurried inside. She looked around quickly and called Lindsay in.

"Did you see anything?"

"No, nothing," answered Lindsay. "What was Brandon doing?"

"I don't know. Let's go check it out." They walked to the back door and unlocked it so Brandon could come in. He was walking back from the corner of the yard.

"What were you doing?" hollered Lindsay.

Brandon motioned for them to be quiet and he hurried inside and closed the door. "I saw someone standing on the sidewalk behind those vines that are all wrapped around the fence."

"The honeysuckle vines?" asked Chelsea.

"Ya, I guess," he said. "Anyway I ran around back so I could see who it was."

"Who was it?" asked Lindsay with wide eyes.

"Mrs. Norris," he answered.

"Mrs. Norris," both the girls repeated. "What was she doing?"

"Eavesdropping," said Brandon. "I'm sure of it."

Just then they all heard Tabby meow. Lindsay called for her, but she didn't come. The meowing continued. They spread out and all started calling for her.

"I think it sounds like she's upstairs," said Chelsea. They all walked upstairs calling for the cat. She answered their calls but they couldn't find her anywhere.

"She isn't up here," said Brandon. "We've checked all the rooms and closets." They stood in the hallway and listened for her again.

"It sounds like she's downstairs now," said Chelsea. They went back downstairs and checked in every place they could possibly imagine. Brandon even opened the cellar door and called for her.

"Maybe she is playing with us," said Lindsay. "Let's fix her food and see if she comes to eat."

That didn't work either. The cat continued to meow and the kids continued to look for her. Brandon was still looking downstairs so the girls went back up to check the bedrooms again. They walked quietly listening intently to her cries and trying to track them. They found themselves in Mr. Hunter's bedroom.

"I'm sure she's in here somewhere," said Lindsay. She opened the closet door again. Tabby's meow sounded even louder once the closet door was open. Chelsea and Lindsay stared into the closet.

Mr. Hunter's clothes were hung neatly. Several dark colored suites hung to the left. The girls both remembered seeing him wear those suites on Sunday mornings. Next to the suits were some neatly pressed pants and several white shirts.

There was a shelf at the top of the closet which held several boxes but nothing Tabby could have gotten herself into. On the floor of the closet were Mr. Hunter's shoes. Two pair of dress shoes, house slippers, one pair of tennis shoes and a couple of boxes, probably containing old shoes he hadn't worn in awhile. Tabby's meows could still be heard very clearly.

"Chelsea," said Lindsay inquisitively. "Do you notice anything unusual about those shoes?"

"No."

"Notice how the ones on the left are lined up neatly but these on the right are kind of bunched up, like they were thrown in."

"So, my closet looks like that."

"No, in your closet all the shoes are messed up, not just one side," she said thoughtfully.

"So, what's your point?"

"I don't know, I just think it's strange," she said.

Brandon came into the room about that time. "Did you find her?" he asked hopefully.

"Not yet," said Lindsay, "but she's in this room, I know it."

Lindsay was inside the closet now.

"Did you look under the bed, Chelsea?" he asked.

Before she could answer Lindsay let out a blood curdling scream, and jumped from the closet.

"What is it, what is it," the other two ran to her side.

"See that small hole down toward the floor?" She pointed it out on the right side of the closet. "I stuck my finger in there and something scratched me."

They looked down at her finger to see a small cut. They all got down on their hands and knees and looked at the hole closer. Chelsea picked up one of Mr. Hunter's shoes and stuck the shoestring into the hole. A small furry paw came out of the hole to grab the shoe string. They all cracked up.

"How did she get behind the wall?" said Brandon.

"And more importantly how are we going to get her out?" stated Chelsea.

Lindsay continued to play with Tabby through the hole and talk to her. "We'll get you out soon, Tabby. We just have to find out how you got in there."

"Look," said Chelsea pointing up the wall higher. "Another hole." She put her finger in that hole and the entire wall shook.

"Watch out," said Brandon. "That wall must not be very sturdy." Chelsea pushed again and this time the wall moved in a little.

"Chelsea, what are you doing?"

Chelsea wasn't listening. She pushed one more time and that section of the wall moved back enough that the Tabby came running out.

Lindsay stroked the cat again and again. Tabby purred and rubbed against everyone, obviously quite relieved to be free.

"How did you get in there?" Lindsay asked her.

"Brandon, go get a flashlight," said Chelsea. "Let's see if we can see anything back here."

Brandon was back in an instant. "Let me see, let me see," he said, pushing his way into the closet.

"Give me the flashlight," said Chelsea.

"No, get out of my way," he said.

"You guys knock it off," said Lindsay still petting the cat.

"Okay," said Chelsea. "You can look first, but just for a minute." She got out of his way. He couldn't see anything at first. He struggled to get his head in the opening farther. As he did this the wall moved more. He pushed a little more on the wall until he got his head in. He turned the flashlight on and shone it through the opening.

"Oh-my-gosh," was all he could say.

"What, what?" said Chelsea. "Let me see, let me see." She couldn't take it anymore and pushed her way through. As she did so the wall came loose and started to fall on top of them. They both grabbed it and pushed it back up against the back wall.

"Why that's not a wall at all," said Chelsea.

"It's just a loose piece of dry wall. My Dad has several of these laying around in our garage."

By now Lindsay was in the closet again also. "What have you guys done," she said with her mouth dropping open.

"That's nothing," said Brandon. "Look at this." He picked up the flashlight, which had fallen out of his hand in all the commotion and shut off. He turned it back on. Both girls stood staring with their mouths open in amazement at what they saw. A hidden staircase.

"Where do you think it leads to?" whispered Lindsay.

"Do you think it's safe to walk on?" whispered Chelsea.

Brandon stepped onto the first step. It creaked loudly but seemed to be firm.

"I don't know about this, Brandon," said Lindsay. As she said this Tabby jumped out of her hands and ran down the stairs.

"Tabby wait," she shouted.

"Well we have to go down now," said Brandon. "We have to get Tabby."

They took the steps very cautiously, one at a time until they got to the bottom.

"Look," said Brandon. He pointed the flashlight on a pile of chains in the corner next to Tabby. He picked them up and shook them. It was a sound they had all heard before. There was a blank wall at the end of the staircase that pushed open easily. They all stepped out.

"Where are we?" whispered Lindsay.

Brandon shone the flashlight around the room. "The cellar," they all said together.

"Unbelievable," said Brandon. "A real hidden staircase."

"I'll bet it was originally used to hide slaves like Mrs. Lewis was talking about," said Lindsay.

"That doesn't explain how Tabby got in there today," pointed out Chelsea. The cousins looked at each other but didn't say anything. They were all thinking the same thing. Someone besides them had been in the hidden staircase recently. Someone was using it to scare people away from Mr. Hunter's house . . . but who?

"If this was really used for slaves, where would they go from here. Why would a staircase lead them to the cellar unless they could get out of it somehow," stated Brandon. He scanned the basement walls with his flashlight. "There has got to be something else here. You know, another hidden entrance."

"You mean a tunnel?" said Chelsea reading his mind.

"Let's look around some more, we're already down here." They began searching the old musty cellar for any kind of hidden doorway. It was cool down there, but they didn't mind. The temperatures had been very hot lately and Mr. Hunter's house always seemed 10 degrees hotter because it was closed up all day. Besides Brandon's flashlight there was one small window that let a little bit of light in. They moved boxes around and looked in every corner, nothing.

"Maybe they just hid them in the staircase until it was safe," offered Lindsay. "Then they might have gone out the back door at night."

"Maybe," said Brandon, but he wasn't giving up. The only place they hadn't looked was behind the old wine rack in the far corner. "Let's try to move that rack away from the wall," he said. "Maybe we will find something back there."

The three of them tried lifting the rack, but it wouldn't budge.

"This thing must be bolted to the wall," said Chelsea. Just then Brandon got an idea. "Maybe it is bolted to the wall. We were trying to lift it up. Maybe we should try pulling on it."

"I don't know, Brandon," said Lindsay. "I don't want to break anything."

"We won't pull real hard," he promised. "Just a little at first to see if anything moves."

They all three got on the same side and pulled on the wine rack. The wall moved.

"I knew it," said Brandon proudly. "Pull harder."

They all pulled together one more time, but to their surprise it opened quite easily after that, and they all tripped over each other and landed in a heap. Cold air filled the already cool room. As they sat there on the floor looking into the dark tunnel, the door at the top of the staircase opened a little bit. At first they all jumped in surprise. But then

they realized the door was opened by the breeze that blew in from the tunnel.

"That explains everything," said Chelsea. "Someone was hiding in the staircase yesterday when Ms. Carter and her buyers were here. They ran up and down the stairs rattling those chains to try to scare all of us. Then they ran back down them and out through this tunnel."

"And when they opened the tunnel door," Brandon continued, "it forced the cellar door to open and the cold air we felt was actually coming from the tunnel."

"So, now we know how someone has been playing the tricks," stated Lindsay, "but we still don't know who."

Brandon looked at the girls. Then he looked in the tunnel.

"Maybe if we . . ."

9

Against the girls' better judgment, they found themselves entering the tunnel. Brandon was in the lead with the flashlight but they were all very close together. They hadn't gone far when the tunnel went off in two directions. They could either go straight or turn to the left. Without much discussion they went to the left.

"This is a dead end," said Brandon as he swung the flashlight from side to side. The tunnel, which was about five feet high and about that wide came to an abrupt end. As he was about to turn around and go back the other way he noticed something in the corner. It was a small wooden stool. "I wonder what that is doing here?"

"Why would anyone build a tunnel to nowhere?" asked Lindsay.

"Maybe they just never finished it," offered Chelsea. Just then Brandon noticed something up above.

"Look up there," he said. There was some light coming in from up above them.

"That's what the stool is for," said Chelsea. "You have to stand on that to get out. The door is on the ceiling.

Brandon handed the flashlight to Chelsea and moved the stool under the door. Brandon was not quite five feet himself. Fifty-four inches to be exact. He knew that because that is how tall you had to be to ride the Ninja at Six Flags. Every year they went to Six Flags and every year he wasn't tall enough to ride the roller coaster. This year he made it. Just barely, but he made it.

The stool gave him an extra foot or so, enough to raise the door open, but not enough to see out. "This isn't going to work," he said closing the lid back down. "Lindsay, why don't you get on my back?"

Lindsay stood on the stool and got on Brandon's shoulders. Lindsay was almost as tall as Brandon, even though she was a year younger. Chelsea held the flashlight and tried to help Lindsay balance. Lindsay pushed open the door and stuck her head out.

"We're in the garage, I think," said Lindsay.

"Mr. Hunter's garage?" asked Chelsea.

"Ya, I'm pretty sure. There is a lot of junk in here. I'm sure it's his garage. Lower me back down."

Chelsea helped her off of Brandon's shoulders. "Okay, so the first tunnel leads to the garage. If the garage door is unlocked, someone could enter the garage and get into the house through the tunnel," Chelsea said, thinking out loud.

"Ya, they could wait out here until they saw us go into the house," observed Brandon.

"When we get back, let's check the doors to the garage and see if they're locked," commented Lindsay.

"First we need to see where the other tunnel leads," said Brandon who was already headed back down the small passage. The girls followed close behind.

The other tunnel was much longer than the first. They walked for a long time in silence when finally Lindsay spoke.

"How far do you think we have walked?" she asked.

"It seems like miles," said Chelsea. "I can't imagine how long it must have taken to dig this tunnel years ago."

They continued walking in silence. It was cold in the tunnel and Brandon wondered how far under the town they actually were. It narrowed in spots and they would walk single file, then it would get wider again. For the most part it was a very well built tunnel and the thought of it being dangerous never entered their mind. They were on an adventure. With any luck, the answer to this mystery may be just around the corner, and that is all any of them had on their minds.

Finally the tunnel came to an end.

"Look . . . up ahead," said Brandon excitedly. His flashlight was shining on a wooden panel about thirty feet in front of them. Brandon started to run but Chelsea stopped him.

"Brandon wait . . ." she said. "Be quiet. We

don't know where that panel leads to. Chances are it leads right into someone else's basement."

They walked up to the panel cautiously. They tried to listen for some noise on the other side but heard nothing.

"I say we try to open it," said Brandon.

"I don't know if we should," said Chelsea. "We could be breaking into somebody's house. That is against the law you know."

"So what, we go back. What good did it do us to walk all this way if we aren't going to see where it leads?"

"Maybe Brandon's right, Chelsea," said Lindsay. "If we just open it a little and look around, I don't see what that would hurt."

Chelsea thought about it for a minute and then agreed. "Just open it a little at first. Maybe then we can hear something and tell if anyone is home."

"Their hearts were racing as Brandon pushed on the panel . . . nothing. He pushed harder . . . still nothing. They all tried together put the panel wouldn't budge.

Just then they heard something. "Someone's coming," whispered Brandon.

"This old door . . ." They heard a woman's voice say. "I need to get someone out here to work on it. It sticks so bad you can barely open it."

The kids were ready to turn and run like crazy, but something stopped them. Whether it was curiosity or just plain fear they didn't know, but not one of them moved as they heard a door squeak open.

They heard footsteps and then light came through a knothole in the panel. The three of them each took a step back.

"Now where did I put that," they heard a voice say. There was silence for a few minutes. They all recognized the voice immediately but none of them said anything. They were afraid to breathe, let alone speak.

"Oh here it is," she said, "If it was a snake it would've bit me."

The light went off and they heard her going back up the stairs. Still nobody said anything until they heard the door close. Once the door closed, Brandon turned the flashlight on and looked at the girls. They all shook their heads in agreement. "Mrs. Norris!" they said together.

"I told you," said Brandon. "I knew she was eavesdropping on us earlier today."

"That also explains why she is always passing by when we are leaving the house," whispered Chelsea. "She wants to know if we're falling for her little tricks."

"I bet she wants the house for herself," continued Lindsay. "She is always talking about how nice it is."

"She probably thought if she could get the whole town to think it was haunted, Mr. Hunter's son would have to sell it to her real cheap," finished Brandon.

"I wonder how long she has known about the tunnel," said Chelsea.

"Long enough to set up this plan," observed Lindsay.

"Ya," said Brandon, "she's probably been sitting around for years waiting for Mr. Hunter to kick the bucket."

"Well, there was only one problem with her plan," said Chelsea with a smile.

"What's that?" asked Lindsay.

"The Woodland Spies don't believe in ghosts."

They all smiled, proud of themselves for solving another mystery, as they hurried back to Mr. Hunter's house to decide what to do next.

10

They decided not to tell anyone about their findings yet.

"We can't just accuse her," Brandon was saying to Lindsay. "She will just deny it and we can't prove anything."

"You're right," said Chelsea. "We have to catch her in the act."

They had been arguing this point all morning. Chelsea hadn't slept well that night. Since finding the tunnel and the hidden stairway she was much too wired to sleep. Over the past couple of years she had read almost every Nancy Drew book there was, including *The Hidden Staircase.* She thought things like that only happened in books and on T.V.

She had wanted to tell her Mom and Dad all about it, but they had all promised not to, not yet anyway. If they did, they were sure their parents would call the sheriff. They wouldn't be allowed back in the house and they would never get to really solve the mystery. Even though they knew it was Mrs. Norris trying to scare them, they didn't have any proof.

They walked up to the front door and Chelsea put the key in. They didn't bother with their routine of checking the back and side yards. They knew how she was getting in and out.

They walked in and were immediately greeted by Tabby. Lindsay picked her up and began stroking her fur. "Have you been staying out of trouble today?" she asked the orange and white cat. Tabby purred.

"Now remember," whispered Brandon, "don't let on like we know anything while we're in the house." They had talked about this yesterday. Since they wouldn't know whether Mrs. Norris was in the house or not, they wouldn't discuss any plans while they were there.

They fed Tabby and gave her fresh water and then took her out to the garden. "Is it okay to talk out here?" asked Lindsay.

"I think so," said Brandon, "just keep your voice down."

They tossed ideas back and forth about what their next move should be. "One of us could hide in the tunnel that leads to the garage," suggested Chelsea. "Then when she is coming back we could take her picture."

They all agreed that was a good idea but nobody wanted to volunteer to be the one taking the picture. "Besides," said Brandon, "how do we know when she will come back. She has already scared all the potential buyers away. Maybe she won't come back."

They all sat silent for a minute or two thinking about this. "Maybe she left her fingerprints on the chains we found in the hidden stairway," suggested Lindsay.

"Only the police can check for fingerprints," pointed out Chelsea, "and they'll think we're nuts if we go to them now."

They were still sitting there when Brandon looked up and saw Mrs. Norris herself walking down the block. "There she is," he whispered.

"Well, at least we know she's not in the house," said Chelsea.

They all kept an eye on her as she came closer to the house. "I've got an idea," said Brandon, "stay here." He got up and ran around the house. He slowed to a walk as he got to the front yard. He walked out to his bicycle and pretended to mess with the chain. As she reached the corner he got up and spoke to her.

"Hi, Mrs. Norris," he said. She turned to look at him a bit surprised by his greeting.

"Good morning," she replied but continued walking.

"I guess our job is almost done here," Brandon said rather loudly since she was walking away from him. She stopped and turned.

"Why is that?" she questioned.

"Mrs. Carter told us she had the house sold."

"SOLD." She realized she had said this loudly but it was too late to take it back. In a quieter voice she said, "The house is sold?"

"Well almost," Brandon answered, sure his plan was working. "They are coming to look at it tomorrow afternoon around three, but she said they were sure they wanted it. Something about historical reasons."

"I see," was her only reply.

"Most people are afraid of this place," Brandon continued. "The whole town thinks it's haunted."

"Oh . . ." she paused and looked at him with one eyebrow raised. "What do you think?"

"I don't know," said Brandon, afraid he had gone too far with his last remark. "I better get back in and help with Tabby." He turned and walked around the house without saying good-bye. Mrs. Norris watched him go.

Brandon motioned silently for the girls to come back inside the house. Lindsay carried Tabby and they closed the door behind them. He told them about his conversation with Mrs. Norris.

"What did you say all that stuff for?" asked Lindsay.

Chelsea was smiling, "So she would come back tomorrow to scare off the buyers."

"Right," said Brandon. "You know she's going to. You should have seen her face when I told her the house was sold. She'll be back all right, and this time we'll be ready for her."

"Well, Einstein," said Lindsay sarcastically, "that sounds good but you're forgetting one thing. We don't have a plan yet."

"Well, we better think fast," he said. "We only have until three o'clock tomorrow."

They arrived at Mr. Hunter's house around

noon the next day. They had spent many hours going over exactly what they would do. They knew they needed an adult but still didn't want to tell their parents or the police yet. They had called Paul at the church office and asked him to meet them at Mr. Hunter's house at three. They didn't give him any details, they just asked him to come.

As soon as they arrived they went upstairs and pushed Mr. Hunter's bed next to the closet door. This was not an easy task and took a lot longer than they had thought. This would keep her from getting out upstairs. Now for the downstairs.

They went to the basement. There wasn't much down there but a few old boxes full of junk. Their plan was to let her come through the tunnel and into the staircase. Then they would trap her in the staircase until the police got there. It had sounded like a good idea last night, but as they stood in the basement they began to wonder.

"How are we going to trap her in?" questioned Chelsea. "We need something heavy enough that she can't move away."

They picked up several of the boxes. Although they were all heavy, none of them were heavy enough to hold the door closed.

"What if we moved all four of the boxes in front of the door," suggested Lindsay.

"That might work," said Brandon. "I'll go inside and you guys put the boxes against the door. I'll see if I can open the door."

The girls moved three boxes against the door

and told Brandon to try to get out. After several attempts the boxes started to move a little. They placed a fourth box against the door. That time he couldn't get the door to budge. They moved them back and let Brandon out.

"That might work," said Brandon, "but it's gonna be hard for us to move all four boxes without making any noise. Besides, we won't have that much time."

They sat and thought for a few more minutes when Chelsea said, "Wait here, I have an idea."

She ran upstairs and came back with her back pack. "I almost forgot I brought this."

"What's in it?" asked Lindsay.

"Well, I wasn't sure what we would need so I brought a little of everything." She dumped out her back pack onto the cellar floor. String, duct tape, some nails, a pair of pliers, and a hammer fell out.

"Where did you get this stuff?" asked Brandon.

"From the garage. If my Dad finds out he'll kill me, so be careful with it."

"Maybe we should just nail the door closed, once she is inside," suggested Lindsay.

"Oh ya, good idea," Brandon replied sarcastically. "That shouldn't make any noise."

Lindsay gave him a dirty look. "Actually," said Chelsea, deep in thought, "that might not be such a bad idea."

"Huh," said Brandon.

Chelsea took a nail and the hammer over to the panel that led to the staircase. She hammered the nail into the wall next to the door, but just a short way. "Hand me the pliers," she asked Lindsay.

"What are you doing?" asked Brandon.

"You'll see."

Lindsay brought her the pliers. Chelsea grabbed the long end of the nail that was still sticking out of the wall with the pliers. She tried with all her might to bend the nail.

"Oh, I get," said Brandon. "Let me try."

Brandon's attempt to bend the nail was unsuccessful also. "Give me the hammer," he requested.

He took the hammer and wacked the nail a couple of times from the side. The nail bent over across the door.

"There," said Chelsea. "If we put a few more of these in there, that ought to hold her.

"I'm confused," said Lindsay. "Exactly how is she supposed to get in?"

"Simple," said Brandon. "Well twist the nail up, like this, before she gets here." Because the nail wasn't in the wall all the way, it was possible to twist it, so that the bent portion was straight up. "We'll have them all like this at first." He continued. "Then after she goes in, we'll turn them down so that they go across the door." He demonstrated this technique.

"You think that will hold her?" Lindsay questioned.

"It only has to hold her until the police get here," pointed out Chelsea. "Hopefully she won't

even know she is trapped in, until it is too late."

They finished hammering in several more nails and bending them over. They made sure each of them would twist fairly easy. They stood back and observed their handy work.

"Now," said Chelsea, "there is only one thing left to decide." They all stood silent. They knew what it was. "Who is going to hide down here and lock the door after she goes in?"

Silence. "Come on, somebody has to do it."

"Why don't we all do it together," said Lindsay.

"That won't work," said Brandon. "Two of us need to be upstairs pretending we're taking care of Tabby. She'll know something is up if she doesn't hear us."

"Besides," added Chelsea, "someone has to call the police."

"Okay who's it gonna be?" Again, silence.

"Let's draw straws," suggested Brandon. "Whoever gets the smallest straw stays down here."

"Deal," said Chelsea. "I saw some straws in the cabinet upstairs." They followed her upstairs. She got out three identical straws and then cut the end off of one of them with a pair of scissors.

Brandon put the straws behind his back and mixed them up. He placed them in his hand so that the tops were all even and you couldn't see the bottom of them. Lindsay drew first and then Chelsea. They compared their straws. They were of equal length. They looked at Brandon.

"Great," he said, as he stared at the short

straw he was left with. "Okay, I'll hide in the basement and lock the door. No big deal."

He was talking very confidently but the girls looked worried. "Are you sure you can do it?" Lindsay asked.

"I'm sure," he said. "You guys just be making a lot of noise up here so she can't hear me moving around."

"We will," said Chelsea. They looked at the clock on the wall. It was 2:30.

"Let's go back downstairs and find you a good hiding place," said Chelsea.

They went downstairs and found an old tarp laying under the stairs. "I'll cover up with this," said Brandon. "She'll be in too big of a hurry to see me anyway."

"Are you sure you're gonna be okay down here?" Chelsea asked him.

"I'm not afraid." The girls weren't sure if he was trying to convince them or himself.

"You guys better go back upstairs. She might be here anytime."

"Okay" said Chelsea, "but be careful."

They walked upstairs and closed the door. It was 2:45.

They had told Paul to meet them at 3:00. "I hope he's not late," said Lindsay.

They tried to make small talk and play with Tabby but all they could think about was Brandon hiding in the basement, waiting for Mrs. Norris to come through the tunnel and trap her in the staircase. Chelsea wondered if she could have gone through with it if she had chosen the short straw.

It seemed like it was taking forever for 3 o'clock to get here. Chelsea looked at the clock again, 2:55. Maybe she wasn't coming. Maybe Brandon had convinced her the house was already sold and she gave up.

Yesterday that idea would have disappointed Chelsea, but today, at five minutes to three, the thought made her breathe easier. She looked at Lindsay who had been silent for the past five minutes. She was stroking Tabby but Chelsea could tell she was thinking the same thing.

Chelsea got up and went to the window to look out. She wasn't really looking for anything in particular, she just needed to move around. "Maybe we should turn on a radio or something," she suggested.

"There's one on the counter but I don't know if it even works," said Lindsay.

Chelsea walked over to it and turned it on. All they could hear was static. Chelsea was adjusting the knob trying to get a station to come in when the basement door opened just a little bit. Both girls were motionless while a cool breeze blew through the room. Their eyes were wide when they turned to look at each other.

Chelsea looked at the clock: 3:01.

"Call the police," Lindsay mouthed.

Chelsea picked up the phone and dialed the number. She had written it down on a piece of paper but she didn't need to look at it. She held the receiver up to her ear. Her hand was shaking. Was Brandon locking her in? Would she be able to get out before the police got here?

She waited for a ring but never heard one. She hung up to redial. She waited for the dial tone . . . nothing. She clicked the button again and again . . . still nothing.

11

While Chelsea had been dialing, Lindsay had gotten the radio on a station. She turned the radio up louder and whispered to Chelsea.

"What's wrong?"

"The phones are dead," Chelsea whispered back. "Mr. Hunter's son probably had them turned off right after Mr. Hunter died. What are we gonna do?"

With her final words the cellar door slowly opened. Chelsea and Lindsay held hands but didn't move. Brandon stepped quietly up the stairs. He hurried over to them.

"Did you call the police?" he asked. His eyes looked wild and his voice sounded shaky.

"Did you lock her in?"

"Yes. Did you call the police?" he asked again in a shrill whisper.

"The phones are dead," Lindsay whispered back.

His eyes were wide and he took a deep breath. "I'll ride to the police station," he said. "It's just down the road."

The girls were still thinking about this idea

when they heard footsteps coming from the staircase. This was soon followed by chains rattling.

They all knew who it was. They knew where she was. They had even seen the chains on the stairway. But for some reason, they were all terrified.

They ran to the front porch and Brandon was running for his bike, when they saw Paul coming down the road.

"It's Paul; it's Paul," shouted Lindsay, pointing down the road.

Sure enough, Paul was about a block away. He was carrying a soda in one hand and looked up when he heard his name. He had his usual big smile on his face and waved at the cousins, who by now were running toward him.

"Wo, wo, slow down," he said laughingly, as they practically ran into him.

"Come on, we got her trapped inside," said Lindsay pulling on his arm.

"We tried to call the police," explained Chelsea, "but the phones are dead."

"I trapped her in myself," said Brandon. "I hid in the cellar and when she came through the tunnel and went into the hidden staircase I locked her in."

They were all talking at once and Paul was having a hard time understanding any of it. Finally he put two of his fingers in his mouth and let out a shrill whistle. Brandon had tried to master this talent many times but had never been able to. Paul used this technique quite often during their youth meetings at church when things got out of hand. Today was no different, the whistle was followed by silence.

"Now," Paul said. "What is going on?"

They all began to talk at the same time again. Another loud whistle.

"Brandon, you first. What's this about a tunnel?"

Brandon blurted out how they had found a hidden tunnel in Mr. Hunter's house, and that it was originally used in the slave run, but presently being used to scare the daylights out of them. Paul found this amusing.

"I've heard that some of these houses were used in the underground railway, I think that's great that you guys found something."

"Would you listen to us," said Lindsay impatiently. "We have someone trapped in the hidden staircase."

"Let me get this straight," said Paul with a puzzled look on his face. "There is also a hidden staircase?"

The kids were pulling him toward the house as they talked and as they grew closer they lowered their voices to a whisper.

"The hidden staircase leads to the tunnel," Chelsea explained. "Someone has been sneaking in here and trying to scare us into believing the house is haunted."

"Oh good, this ought to be interesting," he

laughed. They could tell he didn't believe a word they were saying.

"Come on and see for yourself," said Lindsay pulling him closer to the door.

Paul crouched down and put a finger to his lips. "Shhh," he whispered. "Let's sneak up on them." He was trying not to laugh but obviously making fun of them. "Do we know who the ghost is?"

"Yes," said Lindsay, "it's Mrs. Norris."

Paul stood up straight and looked at them seriously. "Mrs. Norris? You honestly think Mrs. Norris is in this house trying to scare you?"

"That's what we have been trying to tell you for the last five minutes," said Chelsea.

"You guys aren't pulling my leg?"

"No," they all said together.

Just then Mrs. Norris walked through the iron gate. "What is all the commotion about?" she asked.

The kids all looked at each other in disbelief. How did she get out. Could she have possibly got out the staircase door and through the tunnel that quickly? Maybe she had came out through the garage exit. It didn't matter how she got out. Their chance of catching her was ruined.

Paul looked at them with a half smile and was about to make up some excuse to Mrs. Norris when a noise came from the house. "What was that?" he asked to no one in particular.

The noise came again. "What the heck is going on in here," he said as he stepped past the kids and walked into the foyer. The kids and Mrs. Norris followed. As they all stood in the foyer the sound of footsteps slowly going up and down the staircase could be heard.

"Good heavens," was all Mrs. Norris could say. Then they heard the chains rattling up and down the stairs.

Paul looked at the kids. "You guys aren't trying to pull a fast one on Pastor Paul here, are you?"

"We swear," said Brandon. "Someone came through the tunnel and into the hidden staircase. I locked her . . ." Brandon looked at Mrs. Norris who was standing right next to him. ". . . or whoever, in the staircase. We tried to call the police but the phone lines were dead."

Paul and Mrs. Norris were both staring at the kids. They weren't sure what to think. Just then they heard noise coming from the basement. It was more of a thud than a footstep. It was followed by another and then another.

"They're trying to get out," yelled Brandon as he ran for the cellar door. He was followed by the two girls who had forgotten all about being frightened now that there were not just one but two adults in the house with them. Paul and Mrs. Norris looked at each other with crinkled foreheads. Then Paul shrugged his shoulders and followed the rest of the bunch down the stairs.

As he got the bottom step the door flung open and a person in a overcoat with the hood pulled

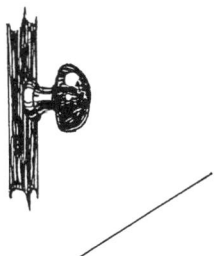

over his head rushed past him and ran across the basement toward the wine rack.

"Get him," the kids all yelled. They were all screaming as Paul leaped for the figure. The villain was quicker than he thought and Paul fell to the floor. He still managed to reach out and grab his foot to trip the intruder. Paul scrambled to his knees and got the bandit by the arms.

"All right, all right, now let's see what's really going on here," he said.

Brandon shone the flashlight on the intruder's hood as Paul pulled it back.

"Mrs. Lewis!!" they all said at the same time.

"Doris Lewis, what in heavens name are you doing down in this basement in that overcoat?" asked Mrs. Norris in disbelief.

"It's all you kids' fault," she said nastily. "I had everyone in the whole town convinced this house was haunted, but oh no, not you three. You had to go nosin' around in things that don't concern you."

Paul had let go of her arms but still knelt on one knee next to her on the floor. "Why did you want the town to think this house is haunted?" he asked.

"None of your business," she said sharply. "Some minister you are. Tackling an old woman like we were playing a game of football. Don't you have any respect for your elders, son?"

She was scolding him as if she had done nothing wrong herself.

Paul just shook his head in disbelief. "With all

due respect, Mrs. Lewis, I couldn't tell who you were. All I saw was someone in an overcoat running across the basement, which leads me back to my first question. What are you doing here?"

"I think it's quite obvious," said Mrs. Norris. "She wanted to buy the house for herself. So she tried to scare off all the potential buyers so the price would go down." Mrs. Norris looked at Mrs. Lewis with a smug smile on her face. "Is that about right Doris?"

"It would have worked too," said Mrs. Lewis as she gave the kids another ugly look, "if it hadn't been for you kids."

Paul looked at the kids with a proud smile on his face. "Brandon, why don't you ride down to the police station and fetch someone for us. I think they might be interested in Mrs. Lewis' story."

Brandon was back in a few minutes with Officer Ryan and Sheriff Akers, who just happened to be at the station when Brandon arrived. Officer Ryan questioned Brandon's story at first but Sheriff Akers told him he better check it out.

They arrested Mrs. Lewis for trespassing and said they would have to call Mark Hunter to see if he wanted to press charges or not. A small crowd had gathered on the corner to see what all the fuss was. Mrs. Lewis looked very unhappy as they put her in the back seat of the squad car. Chelsea noticed Mrs. Norris smiling ever so slightly.

Paul was talking to Officer Ryan and told him

the kids would be glad to come to the station and explain everything in more detail.

"Well I better get goin'," said Sheriff Akers to the kids as he walked back to his own car. Then he turned and looked at Brandon. "Who said this job wouldn't be exciting," he said with a wink.

"Keep us in mind if you run across any other odd jobs," Chelsea called to him.

"Oh, I will," he said, "I will." He walked past Officer Ryan's car and looked at Mrs. Lewis sitting in the back seat. She looked very ruffled, and very unpleasant. He looked back at the kids. And then for no apparent reason, he let out a big belly laugh. It was like he had been holding it in ever since he got there. The kids all looked at each other and shrugged their shoulders. He had almost stopped laughing when he opened his own car door. He took off his hat and got in. Then he looked at Mrs. Lewis again and the laughing started all over again.

The kids watched him drive away. As he turned the corner onto Main Street, they could still hear him laughing.

12

The ice cream shop seemed especially crowded Friday afternoon when the kids walked in. The temperatures had been in the 90s all week, which was normal for July in Illinois, but still hard to take. They spotted Paul at the corner table. He smiled and waved them over.

There were only eight tables in the crowded little diner. Most people just got their ice cream and ate it outside on the picnic tables. But today, everyone wanted to stay near the air conditioning.

"What can I get you kids," the waitress asked as they were sitting down.

"I'll have a large chocolate shake," said Brandon.

"That sounds good," said Chelsea.

"Make mine vanilla," Lindsay added.

"Two chocolate and one vanilla," she repeated. "Just take me a minute."

"So," Paul said as he sat his drink down, "how does it feel to be the town heroes . . . again." He rolled his eyes as he said it, but they could tell he was proud of them.

"We're getting used to it," said Brandon jokingly, "no autographs please."

Paul laughed. "Seriously though, I want you guys to know how proud I am of you. Most kids would have run scared, but you guys really kept your heads. You stayed calm, you gathered clues and then you took action. That took a lot of guts."

The three cousins smiled. The waitress came back with their shakes and set them on the table. They each got their money out.

"Don't worry about it," she said with a smile. "It's on the house."

"Why?" asked Brandon.

"Why? You're celebrities, that's why. Haven't you seen today's paper?"

"We saw it," answered Chelsea. The truth is they had been admiring the article on the front page of the *Sunrise Times* all morning. Brandon and Lindsay's Mom works for the paper and had gotten them a copy first thing this morning. Although she hadn't written the article herself, she probably had some pull as to how it ended up on the front page.

"Enjoy your ice cream," she said with wink.

"Thank you," they all chimed in.

"So, what's next for the Woodland Spies?" Paul asked.

"Well, we still have to take care of Tabby for a few days," said Lindsay. "Mr. Hunter's son called today and thanked us for everything. I guess Officer Ryan had gotten ahold of him yesterday and explained everything that had happened."

"I bet he was surprised," laughed Paul.

"You could say that," said Chelsea. "He can't wait to get home and check out the hidden staircase and the tunnel. He said he doesn't think his Dad even knew about them."

"Well, his Dad wasn't a clever detective."

They smiled and drank more of their shakes.

"So is the house still on the market?"

"No, that's the other thing we forgot to tell you. Mrs. Norris called him last night and they made an agreement." Chelsea talked in between drinks.

"Mrs. Norris really did want the house?"

"Ya, we were at least partly right about her also. I guess her family tree shows that her great-great-grandfather used to live there. The tunnel does lead to her house, but her end has been boarded up for years."

"Did she know the tunnel led to Mr. Hunter's house?"

"She said she suspected that it did only because her research showed that both houses were built by the same man during the same time period. He was very active in the underground railway," Brandon talked as if he should be working in the museum himself.

"It sounds like she must have been doing a lot of work herself."

"Ya, she was," answered Lindsay. "That is why we saw her going into the museum. She's the one who told Mrs. Lewis that some people were coming to look at the house yesterday."

"Oh, so that's how she found out."

Lindsay, who had been quiet drinking her shake, decided to finish the story. "Mrs. Norris didn't think she could afford the house, so she never even approached Mrs. Carter. Mark said he was just glad to see the house going to someone who cared about it and that he knew she would take care of it. The best part is that she agreed to keep Tabby. I would have hated to see Tabby have to leave that house. She loves it there."

Paul looked at all three cousins and shook his head. "So what's next for you three sleuths?"

Brandon sucked up the last of his shake with his straw. "Maybe we'll take some time off," he said. "You know we could use a vacation. School will be starting soon."

"Great, I have just the thing for you."

"What?" they asked inquisitively.

"Camp," Paul said enthusiastically.

"You mean summer camp?" asked Brandon.

"Well, kinda. We take kids to church camp all summer you know. Your age group will be going in just a couple of weeks."

"What do you do there?" Chelsea asked.

"Oh man, all kinds of stuff. We have crafts, games, canoeing, swimming, you name it. We're really trying to get a lot of people interested this year. Attendance has really been low."

"Why is that?"

"I don't know. I guess you could say it is a mystery." He said the last sentence slow to get their attention.

"Did you say, mystery?"